D0106295

DON'T GO INTO THE FOREST!

Veronika Martenova Charles

Illustrated by David Parkins

Tundra Books

JUN 2009

Text copyright © 2007 by Veronika Martenova Charles
Illustrations copyright © 2007 by David Parkins

Published in Canada by Tundra Books,
75 Sherbourne Street, Toronto, Ontario M5A 2P9

Published in the United States by Tundra Books of Northern New York,
P.O. Box 1030, Plattsburgh, New York 12901

Library of Congress Control Number: 2006903144

All rights reserved. The use of any part of this publication reproduced, transmitted in any form or by any means, electronic, mechanical, photocopying, recording, or otherwise, or stored in a retrieval system, without the prior written consent of the publisher—or, in case of photocopying or other reprographic copying, a licence from the Canadian Copyright Licensing Agency—is an infringement of the copyright law.

Library and Archives Canada Cataloguing in Publication

Charles, Veronika Martenova
    Don't go into the forest! / Veronika Martenova Charles ; [illustrated by] David Parkins.

(Easy-to-read spooky tales)
ISBN 978-0-88776-778-4

    1. Horror tales, Canadian (English). 2. Children's stories, Canadian (English). I. Parkins, David II. Charles, Veronika Martenova. Easy-to-read spooky tales. III. Title.

PS8555.H42242D58 2007   jC813'.54   C2006-901936-3

ONTARIO ARTS COUNCIL
CONSEIL DES ARTS DE L'ONTARIO

We acknowledge the financial support of the Government of Canada through the Book Publishing Industry Development Program (BPIDP) and that of the Government of Ontario through the Ontario Media Development Corporation's Ontario Book Initiative. We further acknowledge the support of the Canada Council for the Arts and the Ontario Arts Council for our publishing program.

Printed and bound in Canada

1 2 3 4 5 6   12 11 10 09 08 07

CONTENTS

At the Cottage Part 1   4

Little People   8
(My Story)

Pot Woman   22
(Leon's Story)

Berbalangs   34
(Marcos' Story)

At the Cottage Part 2   46

Afterword   55

Where the Stories Come From   56

AT THE COTTAGE
PART 1

On Saturday afternoon,

our family arrived at the cottage.

My friends Leon and Marcos

were with us.

"It's hot!" said Leon.

"I'm thirsty," complained Marcos.

"Hold on!" I said,

and went to find my mother.

"Can we go to the store

and buy ice cream?"

"Sure," said my mother.

"Buy some ketchup, too, please.

We'll roast hot dogs

on the bonfire tonight."

She gave me some money.

"Be home in time for dinner,

and don't go into the forest!"

When we got to the store,

we bought ice cream and ketchup.

Then we walked to the beach.

Some big kids were playing ball.

"Let's watch!" said Marcos.

"We can't stay for

the whole game," I told him.

"We have to be back by dinner."

"Can't we cut through the forest?"

asked Marcos.

"No, my mom thinks something

bad could happen," I said.

"Like what?" Leon asked.

"The Little People

might get us," I said.

"Who are they?" Marcos asked.

"I'll tell you a story," I said.

★

LITTLE PEOPLE

(My Story)

"Please take these apples

to the market,"

Jenna's mother said.

"Your brother can go with you."

"I don't want to!" said Tate.

"You must help your sister,"

Mother told him.

"But don't go into the forest!

Remember the Little People."

Little People were creatures

who took care of the forest.

If children trampled in the woods,

they would catch them

and chew their fingernails!

Jenna carried the basket

and Tate walked behind her.

Soon they came to a forest.

Tate jumped from the road

and hid behind the trees.

"Get back on the road!

Remember the Little People,"

said Jenna.

"Make me!" Tate called back.

"Come NOW, or I'm leaving

without you!" Jenna warned.

"Good!" Tate said.

"I didn't want to come anyway."

"The Little People will get you,"
Jenna said.

"Ha!" Tate laughed.

"Why couldn't I have a sister
instead?" Jenna sighed.

"I'll pick him up on the
way back," she told herself.

Then she left.

After Jenna was gone,

Tate got bored.

He sat on the ground

and closed his eyes.

"Now we have him,"

tiny voices cackled.

Tate opened his eyes and saw

little creatures leaning over him.

He tried to get up and run,

but he couldn't move.

He tried to scream,

but there was no sound.

By the time Jenna had sold

the apples, her anger was gone.

I hope Tate is waiting

by the road, she thought.

But when Jenna reached the forest,

she didn't see him.

"Tate!" she called. "Let's go!"

There was no reply.

Jenna started to panic.

"It's the Little People!

Tate!" she called,

as she searched the forest.

She came to a thick bush.

Something was sticking out.

A shoe!

"Tate?" Jenna whispered.

She crawled into the bush.

Tate was tied and hidden

under a pile of branches.

The Little People must be

saving him for dinner.

They would be back later

to chew on his nails.

Jenna untied Tate

and helped him to the road.

They ran all the way home.

When they were safe, Jenna said,

"Next time do as you're told!"

Tate said he would, and he did.

★　★　★

"Cool!" said Marcos.

"Do you think that story is true?"

"Maybe," I said.

"There are lots of spooky things in the woods," said Leon.

"Have you heard about the Pot Woman?"

"No," we replied. "Tell us."

★

POT WOMAN

(Leon's Story)

Gil lived with his grandparents

near a forest.

"You can play in the yard,"

his grandparents told him,

"but don't go into the forest!

Years ago, your parents

went in there

and they never came back."

At first Gil did as he was told.

But as he grew older,

he began to wonder:

Why can't I go into the woods?

What happened to my parents?

Finally, Gil went into the forest.

There was a path.

I'll follow it, he thought,

and see where it goes.

He didn't notice

that it was getting late.

Soon it was too dark

to see the path.

I'll never find my way back now,

Gil thought.

Tomorrow, when it's light,

I'll find my way home.

Gil tried to sleep,

but he heard strange sounds

coming from the ground

beside him.

He dug into the dirt,

and found – a skull!

It was talking!

"Listen!" said the skull.

"A woman lives in this forest.

She walks among the trees

carrying a big pot.

She points the pot

at any people she sees

and it sucks them in.

Then the woman eats them.

She eats everyone

who comes here.

She ate me.

She will eat you, too!"

"What can I do?" asked Gil.

"Hide, or the Pot Woman

will find you," the skull said.

All that night Gil dug

in the ground with his hands.

When the hole was deep enough,

he buried himself,

leaving just one eye

and his nose uncovered.

Early the next morning,

Gil spied a woman with a

big pot walking toward him.

She was pointing the pot

left and right.

She passed right over Gil,

and disappeared

behind the trees!

Gil dug himself out

and he ran the other way.

He didn't stop until he was

out of the forest and back

at his grandparents' house.

"You've been in the forest,

haven't you?"

asked his grandparents.

"You're lucky to be alive!

You must never go there again."

Gil promised he wouldn't,

and he never did.

★ ★ ★

"I bet the Pot Woman

gobbled up his parents,"

said Marcos.

I looked at my watch.

"We should go," I told them.

"Wait! It's my turn to tell a story,"

Marcos said.

"This one is about Berbalangs."

★

BERBALANGS

(Marcos' Story)

Chito was walking alone.

He stopped at an inn for dinner.

"Do you need a room?"

the innkeeper asked.

"No. I have to keep going,"

Chito said. "My friend

is expecting me."

"But the road goes through

the woods," said the owner.

"Take my advice.

Don't go into the forest!"

"Why not?" Chito asked.

"There are strange people

living there," replied the man.

"They have eyes like cats.

They are called Berbalangs."

The owner leaned closer.

"At night, Berbalangs turn

into heads with wings

and their eyes glow.

They make loud cries.

But as they get closer,

they become quiet.

When they are really near,"

the owner whispered,

"all you hear is the flapping

of their wings. Then they attack!"

"Nonsense!" said Chito.

"That is a silly story told

to scare children.

I'll be on my way."

It was a warm, still night.

Tall trees stood like giants

beside the road.

After a while, Chito came upon

a few houses.

The lights were on,

but everything was quiet.

He went to one window

and looked in.

Nobody was there, but water

was boiling on the stove.

Strange, he thought.

Then he heard crying.

He looked around.

No one was there.

The crying stopped.

Then he heard another sound.

Flip-flap, flip-flap, flip-flap.

It sounded like wings.

The air around him moved

as if a giant fan was blowing.

Between the trees,

glowing cats' eyes danced

up and down.

Chito began to run.

The eyes were all around him.

Chito reached an open field.

He saw his friend's farmhouse.

Someone came out of the house.

Then everything went black.

When Chito awoke,

he was in a bed.

His friend sat beside him.

"Where are they?" Chito cried.

"Who?" asked his friend.

"The Berbalangs!

They were after me!"

"You must have hit your head

when you fell," said his friend,

his eyes shiny and narrow.

"You're imagining things."

Chito's friend left the room.

Why doesn't he believe me?

Chito wondered.

Something was different

about his friend.

Something about his eyes . . .

There was a cry

from outside the room.

The door burst open

and a cold wind rushed in.

The room filled with sound.

Flip-flap, flip-flap. . . .

★   ★   ★

AT THE COTTAGE
PART 2

"Oooo . . . Oooo. . . ."

Marcos flapped his arms.

"I'm coming to get you.

I'm a Berbalang!"

"Stop that! What time is it?"

I asked.

"It's six-thirty," replied Leon.

"We'd better take a shortcut

through the forest," said Marcos.

"But Mom said not to go there,"

I replied.

"She also said not to be late

for dinner," added Leon.

We all stepped into the forest

and walked for a long time.

But something was wrong.

It was getting dark

and we were still walking.

"Some shortcut," said Marcos.

"Do you really know the way?"

"Yes," I said.

(But maybe I was wrong.)

"Look!" said Leon. "I think

we passed this tree before.

We are walking in circles!"

"I have to think!" I said.

I sat on the ground.

When I looked up,

a woman was coming our way.

She was carrying a big pot!

"POT WOMAN!" I screamed,

and started running.

Leon and Marcos were

close behind.

There was a buzzing in my ears.

I tripped and tumbled.

My shirt was wet.

I was covered in – blood!

"Help!" I screamed.

"What happened?" Leon asked.

"I'm bleeding!" I cried.

Marcos wiped his finger

on my shirt and licked it.

"Ketchup!" he said.

"You popped the lid

when you fell."

I felt much better.

We stepped out of the forest

not far from where we'd started.

A car was coming down the road.

It stopped. It was my mom.

"Boys! Where were you?"

she asked. "I was worried sick.

We phoned the store.

They told us you left hours ago."

"We got lost in the forest,"

I told her. "You were right,

we should not have gone in."

"Well, you are safe now," she said.

She drove us back to the cottage.

The bonfire was burning

and our neighbors were there, too.

"Go and have something to eat,"

said my mother.

I looked at the picnic table.

My heart stopped.

A big pot was sitting there.

"What's that?" I asked.

"We are having a potluck dinner,"
said my mother.

"Ms. Brown brought some chili.
Don't you want some?"

"I'll just have a hot dog," I said.

"Let's eat inside," said Leon.
Mom smiled as we left.

"Hey!" said Marcos. "Did her
eyes look kind of . . . strange?"

AFTERWORD

What do you think happened

to Chito at the end of *The*

Berbalangs? Do you think that the

Berbalangs got him? Is there some

way that Chito's story could have

a happy ending?

WHERE THE STORIES COME FROM

Little People and Pot Woman

are characters that appear

in Native American legends.

Berbalangs can be found

in the folklore of the Philippines.

Throughout the world, many

cultures have stories about scary

beings that live in the forest.

Perhaps adults invented them

to keep small children from

going into the forest alone.